THE SLEEP OF BIRDS (P5.) THE SPOON (P21.)

Sleep of Birds
Tomas Vaiseta

Translated by
Jeremy Hill

Published in English by Strangers Press, Norwich, 2023
Part of UEA Publishing Project

All rights reserved
Author © Tomas Vaiseta, 2023
Translator © Jeremy Hill, 2023

Printed by
Swallowtail, Norwich

Series editors
Nathan Hamilton, Aušra Kaziliūnaitė

Editorial assistance
Senica Maltese

Cover design and typesetting
Glen & Rebecca Robinson (aka GRRR.UK)

Design and illustration © 2023
Glen Robinson, Rebecca Robinson

The rights of Tomas Vaiseta to be identified as the author and Jeremy Hill to be identified as the translator of this work have been asserted in accordance with the Copyright, Designs and Patents Act, 1988. This booklet is sold subject to the condition that it shall not, by way of trade or otherwise, be lent, resold, hired out, stored in a retrieval system, or otherwise circulated without the publisher's prior consent in any form of binding or cover other than that in which it is published and without a similar condition including this condition being imposed on the subsequent purchaser.

ISBN: 978-1-913861-75-9

KŪNAI was made possible by generous funding
from The Lithuanian Culture Institute

THE SLEEP
OF BIRDS

When darkness steals in and thoughts turn to dreams, waves of sleep roll over the seagull colonies. This is not poetry, it is a scientific discovery.

Delfi.lt

It was always like this: what circulated in the Soviet Union as a joke, the West accepted as fact. This phenomenon was reciprocal. Soviet people regarded all Westerners as stupid and rich and believed the half-wits on the other side of the iron curtain always told jokes with a serious expression. The Westerners, of course, were not dim-witted. On the contrary – they tried to find a rational explanation for any absurdity emanating from the Soviet camp, to rationalise the grotesque world of Ubu the King. Thus, jokes, no matter what kind of idiocy they recounted, became not so much a laugh at the table as a challenge of logic to unravel. Neither one side nor the other had an absolute concern for what we'd call truth.

Tomas

This is what happened with the joke about Soviet sex. When one woman excitedly exclaimed that there was no sex in the Soviet Union, no one wanted to hear the end of the sentence and both sides reverted to type. Although it was self-evident that such a claim didn't accord with common sense, my own life accidentally aligned as if to confirm its accuracy. When our country regained its independence, I was fifteen; when the Soviet Union finally fell, I had celebrated my seventeenth birthday, and my virginity still weighed upon me. So it was that a happy historical coincidence came to be: sex came into my life after the fall of the Soviet empire.

We got back after the concert, towards morning – I woke up around midday. The woman lying next to me was still sweetly and happily sleeping. I hear some commotion behind the wall: Kristina and Mantas are jostling in bed and giggling. What seemed unimaginable ten years ago has now become commonplace: a woman has rented a flat with a man. But they aren't a couple. Or to be precise: they aren't a successful couple, but this failure appears to both parties so painless that it is quickly outweighed by the financial savings. I am lying lazily in bed, with the back of my head propped against the wooden bedstead, listening to their intimate rustlings. The metal bed frame squeaks on the other side of the wall, the door of the adjoining room opens and light footsteps float down the corridor: Kristina steps into the bathroom. She seems to be in a hurry. As always, she hasn't put on any clothing, she's wearing only her knickers. It's not difficult to work it out: her hurrying is a fake. She's hurrying, conscious of every ear closely following her steps. My sex swells painfully with blood. Not for the first time, I notice her desire to feel observed – not with the eyes, absolutely not with the eyes, but in the imagination, aided by the senses – sounds, smells, memories. She turns on the tap. She stands in front of the mirror, lifting her curly raven-black hair up in her hands. I see her slender shoulders, her fragile back with a bright furrow between the shoulder blades, her slender, perhaps too slender, torso, her hips covered with thin bluish material, always – always, without exception – squeezed into tight trousers. This is the truest pain that needs to be assuaged. The woman next

Vaiseta

to me starts to breathe shallowly. I stuff my hands under the duvet. I see Kristina's reflection in the mirror: some of the curls have fallen over her forehead, and in this moment of pretend solitude, she delights girlishly in their freedom – her eyes are pale, always appearing to float gently, her lips are thin, without expression. She would like to plump her lips just a fraction. Her chin is pointed but not threatening, somehow meekly transforming into her graceful neckline and beyond, of course, to her breasts, which do not betray any meekness; they are so proud and demanding, almost austere, that, when I stand in front of Kristina, I always feel guilty, as if I've imprisoned two small squirrels in cramped cages with my own hands. At the first touch, my sex stings – I wince, but I don't let my hand drop. I move my hand as gently as I can, so that I don't wake the sleeping woman; however, with the slow movements, I cannot smother the pain, and soon, as my consciousness darkens, it becomes harder and harder to control myself, until eventually all caution and shame leave me with the drops of sweat on my body. I lose control, and the woman next to me seems to wake up: she suddenly opens one eye and closes it again. The mirror cuts Kristina's body off at the waist, just above the belly button, but I could swear that in this depression there is no nodule, there might simply not be one, perhaps there wasn't even a belly button, because Kristina could not be tied by an umbilical cord to any other living being, even if that other being was her mother. She never was, and never will, be attached to this world. She lives more as a reflection of the mirror than as a figure in front of it, more as a promise than its fulfilment, more as a fictional purgatory than a truly existent heaven or hell, and I longed to sink into this merciless fantasy. I am liberated from the pain. An eye opens and closes. A jet of water is flowing without stopping – whatever she's doing now, she's not washing, and most likely this is a signal to the ears which – she knows – continue to listen to her. Kristina – the reflection, Kristina – in the mirror, Kristina – the real, is observing herself with a sweet facial expression, her self-material-body, her representative in this pitiful reality: where Kristina lives, there aren't any walls, and there never have been. She sees straight through our walls, so she can easily watch with dazed eyes, as

Tomas

if behind her back. Without restraining the blast of pleasure aroused from within, I cough as if I'm choking and raise my head uncontrollably from the pillow. An eye opens. And closes. The sleeping woman smiles.

That sex existed in the Soviet Union, I discovered long before the fall of the empire. For what it's worth, I was not yet eleven, which was during the period when perestroika had only taken hold in Moscow. But in our cowering country nobody yet talked about it. Once as a young child, frightened as I often was by who knew what, I wandered through the spacious apartment (which had been assigned to my father, a high apparatchik of the nomenklatura) in search of my mother. After checking all the usual places – the kitchen, the living room, the children's room, even the master bedroom – I couldn't find her anywhere. Only one possibility was left – *my father's room*, which was rarely entered. The door was closed, but I was used to this from an early age – in our home, the family members would, whenever they could, close the doors to shut themselves off from the rest. This didn't, however, mean a single family member would pay any heed to the closed doors, to understand them as a demand from another family member, as if to say, respect my privacy – a closed door was just a door you had to open before entering a room. This collective disrespect of the rule which we had individually created was, for all I know, the factor that most encouraged this practice to consolidate. The door of *Father's room* was closed. Without thinking, I opened it and on *Father's bed*, I saw my father scrambling like a wild beast into his cavernous lair to finish gobbling the day's prey, of which only a head, turned to the side remained; a head that belonged to my mother. Closed doors that could open at any moment. It's no wonder we all felt lonely and insecure at home.

The hair broke off and fluttered down. The sun was burning hot. Its rays cut a vacuum channel in the air, and the hair slid down like a gondola. Its bulb shone like the keel of a boat. The blades sharpened into the afternoon. On a hot day in July, we met, cut off from the air. You suggested having breakfast. I was surprised. We

Vaiseta

were divorced, then you said, I love you, *and I insisted,* It would be better for us both if we were apart. *But I agreed. The blades slipped down our forms as we had breakfast on your balcony. Then we fell like chips of plywood onto the shore of the lake; we stretched breakfast out for the whole day. We looked for a more remote place. You got one leg stuck in the mud up to your knees, and we laughed, perhaps I was even scared, but the mud quickly dried and dropped off. We swam, we watched people, I don't remember what we talked about. I remember what I didn't talk about: you forgot to tell me that, from now on, I would have to live through every season anew – without you, where your fingers are, your permanently freezing tips, the indentations of the little finger pads that can be felt only with the lips, where my saliva accumulates, or where, if I took a sample – now – I would still find an ice floe of my DNA in the narrow grooves of your fingers; my saliva, the spittle of my kiss, would still continue to float on your finger pads – now – when I have lived only two hundred years, only two decades, only two years, only two seasons, only two days, only two minutes, only two moments without you because I closed the door, but after all it was yesterday when I lay at your feet and rubbed your shoulders with pine scent; I didn't see your breasts, I didn't see your belly button, my finger pads slid down your spine, and you, turning your head, frowned with one eye open. The edges of the blades impeded me at least three times, but I didn't complain, perhaps they also impeded you – it's difficult to catch oxygen in a vacuum; walking is like a swamp for people cut off from air. We felt like your leg stuck in the mud. You don't know what channels the sun cuts off as you row. We had lunch. The town was squeakily empty, perhaps the knives were squeaking, but there was only one other person perched in the café, it seemed. We persuaded each other that everything would be fine, we looked at each other as if we were on different gondolas which had already passed each other and didn't know how to go back upstream. In the end, I burst into tears. You didn't understand. Either you understood, or you rowed on further in silence. With our only oar in the channel that was cut. I had to cut this one. I'll cut it as I best as I can. I am only an apprentice, not especially talented. Perhaps, when I cut myself off and leave behind only a labyrinth of*

Tomas

dried out channels, I will no longer love you. But I will already be just a hair that has fallen.

That I emerged from this empire without sex, that I inherited all its worst complexes in the name of morality, I felt every time I masturbated and stared into a handful of whitish liquifying semen, tormented by an oppressive feeling of guilt.

 The only so-called sex manual, which I discovered in my father's *secretaire*, cold-bloodedly lectured about the harms of masturbation, especially for the maturing body. Even amongst the multi-ethnic and multi-genre public of our estate, ominous warnings circulated not to waste all of one's potential in adolescence, because, supposedly, everyone was given a set quantity – given by whom? given by nature? given by the party? given by God? – and the reckless pursuit of pleasure in the early period of life would lead unavoidably to a dreary and boring second half of life, devoid of sexual excitement. With the liquid semen dripping between my fingers and oozing on the parquet floor, I imagined my grim fate because I didn't have the will to deny myself pleasure, even for a day.

I discovered that I was bisexual at twenty-five. So, quite late. A man a few years younger had boarded a trolleybus through the front door and, raising his arms like an orangutan, hung onto the roof handles. He glared at the other passengers freely, impudently, without a care. As if he was the owner of this public transport, assessing how many euros he could pack into his pocket. As the trolleybus rolled steadily towards the station, I felt mildly nauseous. I wanted to be sick. The irritation spread through my chest – as if I could have vomited from my lungs and not my stomach. I wanted to think that it was the behaviour of the man that irritated me. But it wasn't. On the contrary – I was attracted by such a brazen expression of freedom. And not even that. Not that at all. That was not the reason for this feeling. I didn't care a damn about his behaviour – his body, his open, impudently naked body was simply too much: he was wearing tight shorts above his knees, and a short-sleeved T-shirt with a wide collar, while his arms, raised upwards,

Vaiseta

exposed a small patch of skin around his navel – a hairless, shallow hollow. On his left forearm flashed a small tattoo – a bird perched on a branch. To look without looking, to breathe without breathing, to hear without hearing, to blink without blinking, to speak without speaking, all at once you suddenly remember the biological and social functions you've been performing unconsciously all your life, but in an ill-fated moment, they remind you of themselves, and bewildered, you forget which you should perform first. Without concealment, he scanned all the passengers, and his behaviour displayed the primitive need to control the situation, but his gaze, as it took in the perimeter, seemed deliberately to skip over me. If I understand anything about human nature, this primal scene of territorial control was designed to set me apart. And this scared me – scared me into feeling happy, to the extent that a strange man can offer happiness in a half-full trolleybus, grinding towards a bus station. At the penultimate stop, Flowers, he made ready to get off. I didn't hesitate, or I think I didn't hesitate – I remained seated to the last moment, but, just before the doors closed, I jumped out after him. He crossed the street and set off towards the Halle market. I followed in hot pursuit. With a gap of seven or eight steps between us, we crossed another street, turned to the left, and found ourselves in a street lined with homeless people, prostitutes, drug addicts, and, most likely, petty thieves. He didn't once turn around but must have noticed or sensed me. A few dozen metres further, he dived into the deep throat of a multicoloured building between a hairdresser and a small bakery. So I quickened my step to a trot and, catching him in the gloom of the doorway, grabbed him by the shoulder. He turned around and smiled but looked surprised. Why didn't you stop? I asked. He smiled but didn't reply. Why did you make me chase after you? I repeated more severely, although obviously I didn't have any right to reproach a stranger in this way. He waved his hands but remained insistently silent. Why did I have to chase after you like some little puppy? – It was clear how angry I was. He understood: he placed one hand on my shoulder, and – still smiling – jabbed at his lips and ear and shook his head. He was unable to hear or speak.

Tomas

Masturbation is an invention or by-product of civilisation, an invented by-product, an epiphenomenon of resistance to nature through chastity. Masturbation is like ecological sex, satisfaction without irreversible consequences, pleasure without harmful intervention. *Let's save our* virginity might equate to *Let's save the rainforests!* By the time I was sixteen, I had become a hardened ecologist who'd saved hundreds of hectares. I remember January of that year as a time full of anxiety and great tension. It was then that I struggled most with my mutating body, and the outside world – I would say now: even in such circumstances – was of little concern. Nevertheless, the anxiety and tension resonated with this outside world, with its politics, with its aggression, its undying instincts of a dying animal. For three or four days, my father hadn't showed up at home, and my mother, with a distressed expression, kept saying she didn't know *which side he's on*. I cared little for either side, but the anxiety and tension inevitably seeped into me too. My mother didn't sleep all night, and, waking up intermittently, I heard the radio crackling in her bedroom.

When I got up the next morning and crawled into the bathroom, she had gone out to the shops. I felt oppressed by the outside world, which interfered and obstructed the ugly, but nevertheless very personal, battle I was having with my body. I still had one way of rejecting the outside world, and in rejecting it to, for a short time, become allies with the body – so my masturbation only increased.

Morning masturbation, standing in a bathroom on cold tiles, is, for a young organism such as myself at the time, one of the more difficult tasks to perform. I think I took too long and sank back into some state of semi-sleep. I didn't hear my mother return and tramp through all the rooms until finally the handle of the bathroom squeaked and I saw her in the doorway. And she saw me, squeezing away at my sex. She might normally have disappeared as if she hadn't noticed, but, today, you might say, more important matters were at hand. So she didn't disappear. On the contrary – to my utter mortification she marched over and, after staring for few seconds with a look that suggested she in fact hadn't understood at all what I was doing, announced, *Tanks are going up and down the streets!* Then, to my wide-eyed surprise, she hugged me, and burst into tears.

Vaiseta

Before him, I didn't know that men could make love face to face. That men could share biological duties so sweetly, or that they might reject without words, but in fact evenly distribute, all the social and cultural roles between their bodies; rough hands meet with rough hands, impatient kisses – impatient kisses, obscene desires – obscene desires, brute force – brute force, flushed face – flushed face. A physiological democracy of sorts, which ordinarily a man cannot give to a woman or a woman to a man. It had never happened for me like this with a woman: when my sex was taken in his hand and started to throb, and he stroked it, he would soothe it, offer safety, promise protection – as if it were a young bird that had fallen from the nest. With women, I made love loudly: not only she, but also I, would burst out moaning. With him, I made love in a more subdued way, and he would only occasionally let out a sound, like the crackling in an electric socket. There was something fundamentally different between carnal love with a woman and carnal love with a man. Whether this was just the different structure of the bodies, the sexes inviting you differently, different faces of the same nature, or something else, something more subtle, or dangerous, I couldn't work out. Perhaps it was the very contrast that afforded the greatest pleasure. After getting to know a man, and submitting to the strength of his body, I didn't give up on women, as with a monarchy of bodies whereby the crown travels from the hands of the male ruler into the hands of the female ruler and back again, but no danger ever arises for the kingdom itself. To have become unfaithful to the woman I loved, to have slept with another person, I felt like I had to find an explanation for myself. I felt that it lay concealed somewhere nearby, I genuinely felt it. But I couldn't find it. It was strange, but I didn't feel shame. Maybe because I didn't find an explanation, or maybe because I wasn't looking for an explanation. Not he and not she, but the difference between them became somehow the summit of bliss.

Perhaps Soviet people themselves did believe they were living in an empire without sex. Maybe, in the times of Andropov or Chernenko, for example, they in fact felt they had turned into

Tomas

androgynes, perhaps hermaphrodites, who subsequently watched the new inhabitants of the empire emerging with astonishment and wondered with amazement who they were and why they wanted to live in such a world. My childhood memories testify to a certain sexlessness, or maybe it was just shamelessness, of Soviet people: after emerging from the bathroom, my father would lounge around stark naked, and my sister would run up to me and whisper, *Dad has a cucumber dangling again.* My mother too for a long time ignored the differences of the sexes and each Sunday, cleaning day, she would come to scrub my back; until one day, on a regular Sunday, as the fiery voice of Gorbachov echoed from the TV in the living room, when my mother, instead of entering the bathroom without ceremony as usual, knocked and tonelessly warned me, *Put on your shorts.* Previously she brought us up with such an androgynous spirit that my sister and I would happily share the bath in the green enamelled bathroom. But something had changed. Me, the moment, the country. I couldn't be certain.

If I was sincere in telling the woman that I loved her, I felt, I had to leave her, and not so much because it would have been easier to hurt her with a confession, but because I had to keep the hope alive to myself that I was really sincere in having said these words to her in the first place.

We had to separate – there was no other solution. As soon as I woke up, I turned to her, and she didn't understand at all. She didn't want to understand. I spoke harshly, almost aggressively, hoping this would help make her hate me. And she behaved as one might have expected, but this didn't help at all – I couldn't resist. She began to implore me, in tears, to make love one more time – this very last time, what do you care? and driven by a desire to deceive myself, and aroused by a fear of separation, I didn't resist. Her period had started, it was the very beginning, so the most furious, the most frenzied blood, but she reassured me, no, she didn't reassure, she demanded that I ignore it, that I take her, that I tear her to pieces like a vulture intoxicated with the smell of blood, that I swoop down, lick the sickeningly bitter liquid between her thighs, ignore her tears, block out her howls...

Vaiseta

When, after work, she walked down Taurakalnis and waited at the corner of the crossing, I would always think of a seagull perched on a broken pier. Somewhat confused, I stared back at her crumpled nightshirt: the semen spilt onto the dark blue silk now looked like seagull droppings, splashed on the pavement; my sex was gasping for air through the putty of her blood.

With every empire, there are also barbarians perceived to be baying at the gates. Is it possible to imagine barbarians invading an empire without sex? Barbarian warriors thirsting for foreign conquest ravage the towns and cities and seize local women who appear before their crazed eyes like indescribable, shining, pure-skinned fantasies – untouched by male egoism, their bodies meticulously cherished. The women, of course, scream in horror, but perhaps also in a kind of dark amazement: *What are these barbarians doing? Are these unicorns bearing the curse of the gods? Are they monsters exiled from the depths of hell, who have come for women's souls? Or is this death itself entering their bodies?* And what do the men, who have lost the battle and are dying among the blasts of fire, think? Does the image they see deprive them of the will to live anyway? Are they starting to regret not having really lived at all? Would at that moment the foundations of the most chaste civilisation ever fall, would the sky be torn in two and rain with blood?

His habit or liking for leaving the door unlocked drove me to despair. There was no place for Bohemian traditions in the Station region, I thought, but he didn't understand this, or he didn't want to understand. He didn't hear, in every sense. Even more infuriating to me was the fact that he justified his policy of unlocked doors, with which he wanted to emphasize his free – not to say, loose – life, by the fact that he couldn't hear anyone ringing or knocking anyway.

He understood his inability to speak or hear as a sign given to him to live, here and now, an unrestrained, carefree life, without obligation, the safety of which the person who sent this sign would ensure. This is what he lived by – logical flaws, as I saw it, and a deafness towards the logical reference points of life.

Tomas

We had a lot of discussions about this, and he devised an ordinary but ingenious concept – his own tabula rasa. In his small one-room apartment, next to the bed, on three metal legs, stood a barely polished white rectangular writing board on the lower edge of which lay two pens – blue and green. Blue belonged to him, green to everyone else. He was proud of this board. The essential idea being that, unlike in other people's lives, with this board a new conversation would always start from, literally, a completely clean slate. In this way, he explained, he might maintain a perfect relationship with others, one without past grievances.

On this occasion, after freely entering his flat as usual, I found the room empty, the only light creeping through a chink from the bathroom, so I immediately turned to the board, with the intention of writing some question. But I froze – there were blood stains scattered on the floor. Traces of blood led to the bathroom. I burst in and found him slumped on the covered toilet. A dark red slit was gaping in place of his mouth, a pool of cherry-red liquid had collected on the tiles. I rushed up to him and, as I stumbled, started to ask – Who has done this? Who has done this to you? – *completely forgetting his inability to reply, his inability to say anything at all. His gaze remained apathetic, unexpectedly cold. I longed to waken him: Don't live in this region, I beg you, promise me you'll get out of here, I think I implored him in much the same way as I had previously. It had been the only time I felt for him not longing but pity, sympathy, a mixture of guilt, anxiety, and loss.* He had assured me several times that life in the Station region, according to the words written on the tabula rasa, suited his spiritual needs. Street love, mud, physical threat, the permanent flux of migrants, the Blessed Virgin Mary – everything together, everything around him, everything inseparable, and he was the same. I reproached him for reading too much Jean Genet; he smiled, but didn't leave any answer on the board, and instead wiped it clean.

I kissed his disfigured mouth, not knowing or thinking whether I was causing him more pain. He remained lifeless. I took stock and began to look for something to help him, in the first place, some tissues at least. And then, finally, I turned my attention to the basin next to me, on the rim of which lay a razor blade soaked in blood.

Vaiseta

My first time can't really be taken as irrefutable proof of the existence of sex in the Soviet Union. On one hand, the Soviet Union, as I have mentioned, was by then smouldering in ruins. On the other, my first serious woman, with whom I hoped to transcend all the thresholds of pleasure, adhered to all the worst, as I thought at the time, traditions of the older morality, such that, more than once, I had to postpone the first time in an attempt to not offend her noble feelings nor upset the image she had fostered as to how things should be. After a while, a vivid hellscape simmered in my eidetic, adolescent mind, especially at night. When at last the fateful moment arrived, when I saw before me a young, slightly trembling, naked woman, I experienced my first time with a woman, but also without her. In the sex manual I found in my parents' desk, this ambiguous situation was described as premature ejaculation.

It was one of the rare Fridays when the woman and I stayed at her home, instead of rotting away in some sleazy bar. So on Saturday, we woke up quite early. We woke up in different ways: she, even after sleeping as much as ten or eleven hours, could always fall back into her dreams, whereas I, rolling my eyes up, noticed how the daylight brightened the white ceiling. I could hear rustling behind the wall, too early for Mantas and Kristina as a pair, lacking the usual intimacy, so I concluded that Mantas had spent the night alone. He got back later than us, we were already asleep, but, without Kristina; he didn't like to linger in bed on mornings like this and would start to bustle about from an early hour. The clatter behind the wall soon stopped, mindless of the noise created by his steps, he shuffled into the bathroom. He was a conceited, egocentric peacock, a typical representative of the male sex, a standard of self-love that from a young age drives women crazy, so he always had the right to choose, and chose the best of the best. Like Kristina. I had never seen him in the bathroom, but I had no doubt that, before starting to wash, he spent at least ten or fifteen minutes standing in front of the mirror admiring himself. He indisputably loved his own body, but I guessed that, like all egocentrics, he was also not completely happy with it, and so a long look at his reflection in the mirror was for him the equivalent of a

Tomas

meditation, when all bodily imperfections disappeared, and in his thoughts he released his perfect 'I', the perfect 'I', which to him was the body and only the body. Mantas's young, constantly polished body – I tried to imagine his morning ritual, taking his sex in his hands. Awakening in me was the same longing for a physiological democracy,. With slow movements of my hand, I returned to thoughts of a man's embrace – movements which served as a request to take me. I really was not mistaken: Mantas had long since slipped into the bathroom, but I couldn't hear any gurgling of water. If he came home without Kristina, he probably spent yesterday evening without her, which means, surrounded by other women, so this morning he could measure the gaze of each one on his body, and hypnotise himself with the victories which didn't exist but could have. It was no less pleasing for me to contemplate his victory: at that moment, Mantas truly could not have imagined that, in the next room, lying under a warm duvet, another man was surrendering to him, but if he had learnt of our rapprochement, he would have experienced it as the greatest defeat of his life, and this thought of a secret joining us without his knowing, which affords pleasure both to him and me, but for the present has not and cannot be revealed, brings me closer to an intoxicating, silent bliss, which the eye watching next to me met with a gushing tear.

THE SPOON

Two days later, they told me that *Vilė* had died. My eyes literally went black, I gasped for breath, I almost fainted. I was sitting at the desk in my office. I leant my elbows on the tabletop and buried my face in my cold hands. *Vilė* was dead. That I understood very clearly. She was no more. But as soon as we learn of a person's death, we immediately doubt that they ever existed at all. And our own life starts to seem a fiction. That is what causes unbearable horror at moments like this.

Vilė was so young.
When they brought her in, lying on a roughly-hewn pine board, she appeared like a thin, soft sliver of pine. Her body wasn't moving, only her head turned. She uttered something in a muffled voice and seemed already half-dead, delirious. But as soon as the nurses tried to change her; she shuddered as if she'd suffered an electric shock. Her clothes were completely tattered. Only the caked mud appeared to be keeping the rags on her body. It must have hurt when the nurses attempted to take off her clothes because she tried to resist. But she had no strength at all. I was on duty that night and I wasn't happy to see the nurses openly laughing at the poor girl's efforts to keep herself covered. No one in the reception area thought of that. Just another victim of a night-time attack. She's out of her head. But I thought, behind the haze shrouding her eyes, there was a glow, a bright flame of self-preservation. I caught sight of a tall man with a ruddy face in the doorway. He gave the name of the girl to someone and immediately disappeared. I later realized it was her father.

Tomas

The psychiatric wards were overcrowded. We sometimes laid the patients down two to a bed and in the gaps between on crumpled mattresses stuffed with straw. One of them had only to groan more loudly or start jibbing, and the silence in the ward would instantly collapse like a house of cards. A dreadful hubbub would break out, and the patients would begin to pinch or kick each other. Then we wouldn't be able to manage without additional doses of aminazine. There was a shortage of air – as if drawing poisonous sulphur into our nostrils, but we couldn't open the windows. The patients emptied themselves in their beds and the nurses didn't have time to change the sheets – though I heard one say: Let the shitheads sleep. The doctor didn't have time to see to everything. Probably at nights no one changed the bedding. I wandered through all the wards of the department. The situation was just as tragic everywhere. It's strange, but only that night did I think about the deplorable conditions in which we keep and try to help the most unfortunate. I could not put Vilė down next to the others. Her shrivelled spirit would immediately be crushed by the heavy air or her body shattered by the kicking of the patient next to her. I told them to place a mattress in the corridor where several other moaning, ghostly people were laid out.

After three or four days, Vilė recovered. She returned to the light, as we would say. Then I noticed her face: pale, marked by purple rings under her eyes, but beautiful, full of youth and freshness. The only disturbing aspect was her stubborn silence.

In the midst of this turmoil, you're on your own. I have worked for twenty years in a madhouse: the shrill clamour, the shrieking, the moaning, the coughing, the crawling, the knocking, the clatter of plates, the muffled, extended bellowing, the uneasy silence – here there is so much of humanity, and it is so real, that you are left only with loneliness. Whenever I caught myself thinking like this, I would force myself to get a grip, to brace myself, to remember my vocation – to help people. But I was never able to do this absolutely, to give myself completely to my work, because each patient – recovered or not – only reinforced a deep sense of loneliness. In this madhouse, I felt as if I was squeezed into the corner of an empty room, seeing the door open but incapable of walking through it. Simply incapable. Or as if I was on a boat which, sailing away from the shore, dissolved into the oblivion of the green-blue sea.

After several better days, Vilė relapsed. She would sink into a state of lethargy which I found difficult to explain because it would then just as quickly pass. A day or two later, she again returned to the world. Her eyes followed the people moving around her; she would let herself be fed and she seemed to be listening carefully to the chatter of the nurses and sisters. Vilė aroused their curiosity, and they competed to be the first to merit the patient's favour. It was folly, but I surmised that other people's attention could help her. Besides, having won their support, Vilė would be safe from the orderlies – in all my years of service, I never met one who understood their job properly.

It wasn't until later that I realised, in observing this competition between the nurses, I was simply envious. Very reluctantly, I had to admit I'd been drawn into this myself. I looked for ways for Vilė to notice me before the others. What was this? Why should the attention of a person who was half-senseless – who barely had a grasp of reality – matter to me? Were the sisters asking themselves the same question? I didn't feel any magic, any heavenly attraction or miracle, which would help me answer the question posed with a cold mind: What was this? What was going on?
    So on the ward visits, I didn't accord her more than a second: these were my tactics. She herself – yes, Vilė herself – had to beg attention from me, only in this way could I win her.

Vilė was still lying in the corridor when a place by a window became free and someone had immediately pushed her into it. Behind the barred glass, the July sun was shining. Unobtrusive, descending. But when the rays began to caress Vilė's body, she began to breathe more deeply, as if her lungs needed the warmth of the sun more than air. She was eating quite well, but she

Tomas

hadn't put on any weight. True, the darkness under her eyes was softening. Her gaze continued to catch signs that were invisible to us, but her face was becoming more attractive, more expressive, eager to say something to those around her, but unable to find the words, not knowing how to translate those signs into a communicable language. Sometimes other patients would slide up to her. I didn't notice any of them trying to harm her, although such things happened in the hospital. But nor did they succeed in forging any closer link, even a very weak one. Her language was not their own.

I don't recall whether I spoke about this with my colleagues, but I assure you that, between us doctors, this had become commonplace: we all envied the patients their solitude. Not the solitude experienced by all healthy people – each of us had too much of this. But of the sort experienced by them, the insane, so sharply and painfully that it begins to arouse infinite joy, exhausted to the last drop and opening up an intoxicating fullness, expressed in such outbursts of delirium and anger that you cannot help but believe in its authenticity and purity. Not a single doctor doubted this: the insane were superior to us in their solitude. We wanted to touch on the solitude of the insane.

Did I really see that? Now I would stake my life it was really so. I wouldn't hesitate for a moment. In the twilight of a gloomy afternoon, she was lying stretched out like other shadows. I was going about my own business, I think I was even hurrying, and only out of habit or instinct, or perhaps because of my sluggish brain, I didn't perceive but only felt a deeper, subdued feeling stirring within me, echoing from depths which are scarcely fathomable, which forced me to glance in Vilė's direction. In this half-light of dusk, you couldn't have seen anything, but I saw – I saw her face, lifeless as usual, in a state of semi-sleep, raw-boned, melting in the vanishing day – and it spoke to me without words.

I cannot forgive myself for not thinking of this sooner. In the left wing, at the other end of the second floor, a few steps past the

Vaiseta

communal washroom, in the far corner, there was a poky, unused room without any clear designation. The patients must have long ago discovered it (probably looking for somewhere where they could be apart from the others), since, when I went there to follow up my recollection, I found it dreadfully scruffy and covered in rubbish and the sort of things you would really not expect to find in a hospital. When Vilė spoke to me, when I finally won her over, I had to change something. For all I know, everything was natural: the recollection of this place had flashed through my memory at the very moment when Vilė spoke. Her language was the language of my memory. This was our salvation. I told them to clear out the room and move Vilė into it. They just about managed to squeeze in the mattress. But I believed that Vilė would be happy.

Now I could visit her without being disturbed by anyone. And see who else was visiting her. I noticed that one nurse dropped in more often than necessary. So, as if incidentally, I slipped in as well. An elderly woman (she had been working here a very long time) was talking to Vilė's silent face. Whenever she saw me, the old nurse respectfully withdrew, but her whole demeanour betrayed a particular pride – she believed that she had forged a special connection with Vilė. This seemed to me an illusion, an impossibility, I didn't see anything in Vilė's face that could confirm this connection, it was difficult even to tell whether she could distinguish that we were two different people, and not a single whitish mass in front of her eyes. When I was on duty, I liked to visit Vilė in the evenings, after dinner and the last injections. She would immediately come back to life, her gaze brightened up – I joyfully acknowledged that, after spending three weeks in hospital, she had noticeably recovered, her treatment yielded better and better results. It was possible that, together with her consciousness, her speech too would start to return to her body. And I recorded all these signs precisely in the evenings when I visited in order to soothe the solitude of both of us.

One day the miracle happened – Vilė spoke. To be fair, I should say that this was only considered a miracle by those who had not been

Tomas

following her daily behaviour. But by now there was no one doing this apart from me. The hospital rejoiced in local miracles. So the first words uttered became the surprise of the day – it became the talk of the staff of other departments, who previously had probably neither seen nor heard anything of Vilė. The secluded room on the second floor of the left wing became the most visited place for a few days. This seemed unacceptable to me; I was angry that the patient's health was being ignored, yet curious orderlies would come to look at Vilė as if she were a museum or circus exhibit, a talking monkey or the like, though no real miracle had happened: such patients often spoke with the passage of time. But Vilė (I understood throughout this fuss) had somehow managed to create her own legend – this sometimes happened here – and this stirred the imagination of the entire staff, maybe even a number of patients.

The old nurse began to display an unnaturally elated mood. I understood this to be her way of rubbing in her victory: Vilė had uttered the words to her. That Vilė spoke to her was, of course, a complete coincidence. To think otherwise was the self-deception of a batty, feeble-minded woman. While I had thought previously that other people's attention might be good for her, I now began to fear that such a whim from a deluded old lady might demonstrate a potential instead for it to do her harm.

In this madhouse, there were endless rules. We used to call them 'the rules of the game', because they were created mainly for the amusement of the staff, as opposed to the running of a smooth operation. In reality, there wasn't just one game, but rather dozens, even hundreds. For example, in disregard of constant warnings and prohibitions, the orderlies would play a form of what they called 'chess'. They would allocate roles among the patients of the two wards – pawns, rooks, bishops, knights, the queen and, of course, the king. Then, through antagonising the poor mental patients into winding each other up and losing their heads, they would wait to see who knocked out whom. Unfortunately, often even in the true sense of the word. It was possible for the king to be 'slain' only after all the other 'pieces' had been knocked out. Another game

Vaiseta

was played in which – probably due to the deadly dreariness – I can find no other explanation – most of the staff got more directly involved. It was called Guardian Angel. At the end of the month, from a common lot, everyone drew out a small piece of paper with a challenge written by other employees. These ranged from the quite innocent to the quite disgusting: say, dressing in lice-ridden clothes, swallowing a standard dose of aminazine, or spending the night in the same bed as a psychologically disturbed patient. The only way to escape the task yourself was to train a patient to willingly perform the allotted challenge for you instead. Such patients were called 'guardian angels', hence the name. I feared this was perhaps the intent of this loathsome old woman with regard to Vilė.

I continued to visit Vilė almost every evening. I tried through my presence not only to offer her as much tenderness and peace as possible, but also to ensure that she didn't get drawn into such silly games.

My premonition of something bad proved correct. I had supposed that, with each day, Vilė's condition was improving. She spoke sparingly with me: she would answer questions either 'yes' or 'no', yet with the old nurse or other staff members she would be more chatty, albeit not very coherently, as if the voice or the thought itself was connecting intermittently. But, one morning before noon, from the far corner of the hospital, I heard shrill cries piercing the air with merciless beats. Shot through with worry, I hastened to Vilė's side. I found her surrounded by orderlies who were trying, with all their might, to keep down a body, Vilė's body, with flailing arms and legs. The old nurse stood stiffly nearby, her face distorted with fright. They didn't succeed in repressing her, though four men were leaning on her and holding her down. I had to inject her with aminazine. Still she didn't calm down – displaying inconceivable strength. She was as powerful as a wave churning beneath four huge sailing vessels. I didn't have any choice: I administered a larger dose, which would be hard for her frail body to endure. Vilė thrashed about for several moments longer, then suddenly went limp and, as with the start of the ebbing tide, all the strength we'd just witnessed receded.

Tomas

The attack did not recur. Vilė became much more irritable. Admittedly, there was a fear that she might lapse but this did not materialise. However, she again became mute, and reacted much more nervously to any person who entered her room. She wouldn't allow the old woman in, for example, and she was now again completely indifferent towards me.

I had to overcome this. The first time I had won Vilė over with my own feigned indifference. The second time, I surmised, I had to win her with my attention. I persisted in visiting her every evening, spending at least an hour by her side, sometimes even two. I tried unobtrusively to strike up a conversation and otherwise prove my goodwill.

I stayed patient, and for this I was rewarded. I had simply misunderstood Vilė's indifference. After six or seven days or so I realised that through such behaviour she was again trying to set me apart from the others. She was sending me signals which I, a fool, failed to quickly grasp. I still couldn't manage fully to figure out what had happened on the morning of the attack the old lady had visited, but I didn't doubt now that the calmness Vilė showed towards me was a conscious decision – a protest against the others and an invitation, a request, perhaps even a plea. Directed at me.

It was difficult for me to admit, it is difficult to speak openly even now, after all, Vilė was in my – and in other's – eyes only a poor patient for a long time, crossed by fate. I tried to explain all the feelings she aroused in me in terms of her need for parental protection or care. I had long ago convinced myself that she was more fragile than the other patients, that her condition required more careful supervision, that her youth was begging for more sincere assistance. But day by day, or, to be precise, night by night, in fact, for the whole of August, in the company of the waning summer behind the window, we were no longer only doctor and patient, only father and daughter, only two strangers who were brought together by chance, for a brief moment. Every evening when I went to Vilė, I felt guilt and was determined to beg

Vaiseta

forgiveness not only from her, but also from the mouldy hospital walls, from the suffocating smell that permeated everywhere, from the excruciating noise of the wards. However, when I saw Vilė's face afresh, I humbly admitted that a stronger force had intervened: I loved Vilė, and Vilė loved me.

The silence of our love counterbalanced the chaos of our surroundings. Through muteness, we pushed back against the unavoidable existence of other people, which – I saw that Vilė felt the same – was reflected in us through our sense of loneliness. Although I well knew a person's inner world and could with a cold mind set out all the stages of the development of love, I could not apply anything similar to the feeling of it. It fell outside the laws determined by science, any schemes which explained reactions, or any dictionaries of medical and psychological terms. Our love called out to us. Vilė's eyes burned – I would swear on my mother's grave that it were so.

Our love could not be embodied in this cramped room without doors, as small as a pea, open to all people and at all times. The only opportunity we might have was a weekly check-up in my office. I prepared for this especially thoroughly. I examined Vilė's face very attentively. Everything was clearly written down. Doubt faded and disappeared. Stroking her forehead, I asked for a little patience. She seemed to understand and waited.

That afternoon the same old nurse was working with me. Having examined one patient, I told the old woman not to take her straight away to the ward, but to accompany her for at least twenty minutes on a walk outside – the weather was, fortunately for us, suitable for this; the tepid sun was wrestling with the cool air of early September. I let Vilė in and lay her on the couch. Again I looked into her eyes – if either of us had doubts, it was me, but she immediately assuaged my thoughts and, without the flicker of a single muscle on her face, invited me closer. I leaned over to kiss her and only then I felt her body shaking – the winds of desire swept through her. I melted and gave in to the pleasure of the moment, which appeared to take hold of Vilė – I didn't fully expect this – even more quickly

Tomas

than me. Whispering an oath of love, I lay down next to her and with gentle motions, accompanied by Vilė's quivering, I opened up her dressing gown and slipped off her knickers. My little Vilė, the frail sliver of pine – by way of her silky skin. I came to her, when suddenly the door opened and the cursed old woman popped up in the doorway. 'Bring me a spoon!' – comrade docter screemed like a wild animal like I erd at ome in the forest comrade docter went on chokin comrade docter slammed the door e suddenly stabbed into me a great pain shot right threw my guts like a red ot poker pulled from the oven and stuffed right in me I dint have the strength to screem I lost all my strength only comrade docter moments later rolled off and I sees that all my crotch is cuvered in blood I urt like ell I wanted to cry but I dint cry I wos only dyin for comrade docter to stop lyin next to me e is now lyin next to me and goin on pantin loudly I still wanted to vomit cos this pantin made me sick Id erd this pantin evry nite now solong I felt it on my face and always wen ther is this pantin it makes me sick and then I always wanna vomit but now my guts urt like ell and my crotch which wos filfy warm blood is pourin from evryware wotll appen to me now I dint understand wotll appen now and wots goin on god as no pity for me I asked god for solong that comrade docter wount come to me wot does e want wot does e want wotever e wants I cant give im I thort if I guessed wot e wanted he woud no longer come cos e always came wen I wos ere and e always came I cant say how long cos I cant say wen wen an ow I got ere ware my dad is I waited at ome for my dad an then I wakes up in a dark coridor cos I ear some woman cryin but I dint get up I dint find my dad only the woman wos very cold she cryed I wos cold too the sun comes out later by the window ware the woman is cryin but the womans disappeared an the sun came out it wosnt cold only wen comrade docter came I wos shakin tho it wosnt cold e came moreanmore another woman dressed in wite smiled at me she laffed she talked she laffed she smiled it wos awful wen comrade docter looked at me the nice woman she closed the door wen comrade docter screemed like a wild animal I spoke to er cos I wanted to smile I wanted to laff lots I wanted to give er appiness cos she gave me appiness she came an smiled wen comrade docter dragged me off to that corner ware e woud come

Vaiseta

at nite an pant e put is ands under the duvay e fumbled with is and an panted on my face evryware I felt ther wos rats runnin under the duvay thats wot comrade docters and wos like wen I wosnt afraid to look at im I asked im to stop e dint stop nite after nite an e woud come then I says to the nice woman with the wite coat comrade docter comes at nites can e not come cos e makes me sick I wanna vomit Im afraid of im the nice woman looked at me she looked she stroked she stroked an says Im a poor litel thing I dreams up all kinds of nonsense that Im talkin cos comrade docter helps me and that I shount talk nonsense she stroked she stroked I got mad I says the docter lets rats under the duvay its so orrible Im afraid but the nice woman goes on stroking me and I shount talk nonsense I coud cry then I coud cry an punch the nice woman in the face I punched an I cryed I cryed lots the men fell on me comrade docter came it wosnt nite but e came emenazin e shouted emenazin an I waited for dad at ome I dint get up I dint find dad wen I wakes up the nice woman comes I dint smile at er no more an comrade docter panted arder an arder e looked e panted e fumbled is and e asked me again I dint understand I wanted to vomit wen e asked an panted as soon as I erd e comes I dint get confused with no one wen e comes I wanted to run away but I ad no legs my legs an ands were someone elses comrade docter comes an says Ive cheered up that Im quiet an its good that Im quiet that were both quiet cos evryones quiet lots of rats fly under the duvay and god evryones quiet so comrade docter nite after nite after nite then says come to me again in my office so our loves quiet Im really fritened so e smiles like the nice woman an says thers notmuchlefttowaitforourlove I went in the nice woman went out the comrade docter laid down so e wos pantin and made me sick sick strait off I wos shakin all over and I begged no more rats e panted in my ear the door slammed an the red ot poker tore my guts pool of blood warm got bigger it wos bad I waited for dad all the wild animals in the forest were waitin for dad I lay filfy nite it wos day again nite an day my guts urt terrible I begged it not to urt day nite quiet evryones quiet my guts really urt mycr otch wa s filfy till I begged it not to urt still the same poolnewpool blood ran day nite day an nite it so urt an warmblood al ways round my legs an burns my guts an then I died.

KŪNAI, meaning 'bodies', is a series of five chapbooks showcasing writing never-before-seen in English from a diverse selection of the finest contemporary writers and translators working in Lithuanian today.

It is the result of Strangers Press' latest exciting collaboration with an international group of authors, translators, publishers, designers and editors, all made possible by generous funding from The Lithuanian Culture Institute.

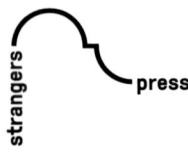

University of East Anglia

NORWICH
UNIVERSITY
OF THE ARTS